KT-562-002

Disney PRINCESS

Enchanted Stables

pi kids®

publications international, ltd.

Cinderella and her horse, Frou, are competing in the Royal Horse Show. It looks like Frou is sure to win! Do you see some of the awards he might receive around the horse-show arena?

Blue ribbon

Pink ribbon

Gold medal

Plaque

Wreath

Trophy

Yellow ribbon

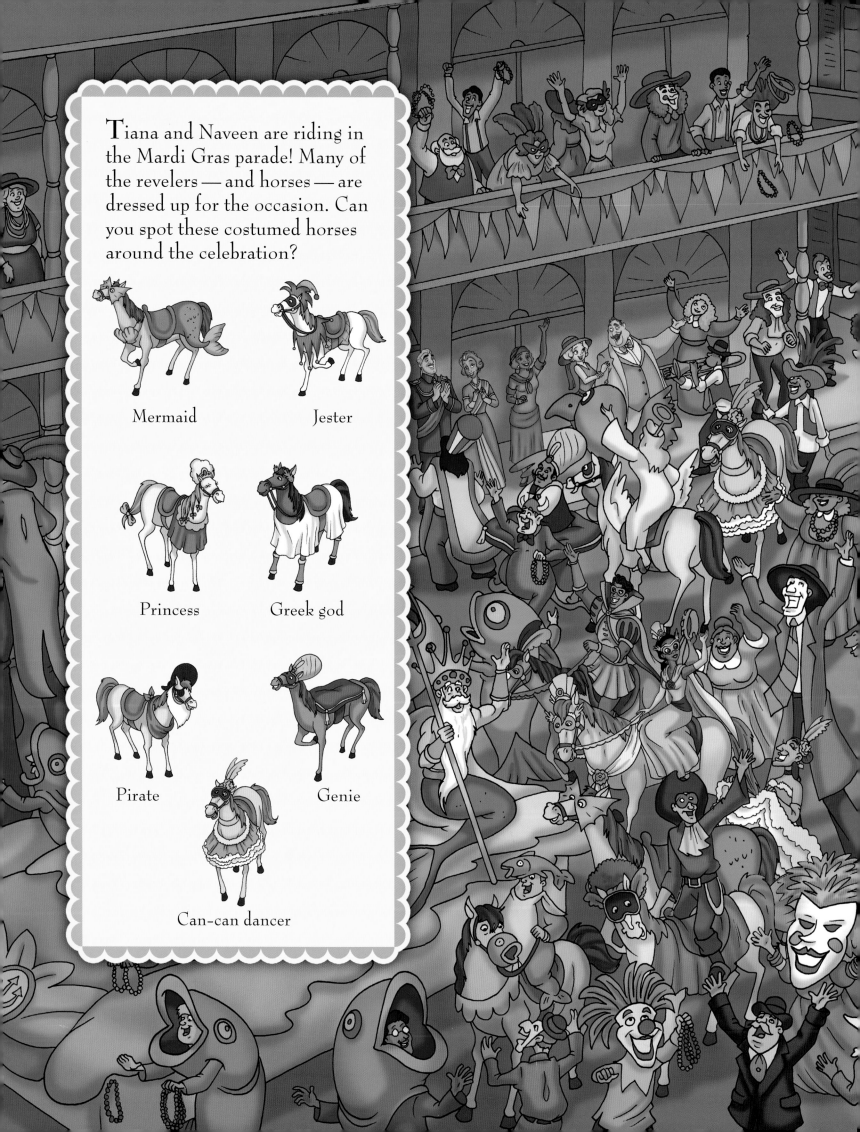

Tiana and Naveen are riding in the Mardi Gras parade! Many of the revelers — and horses — are dressed up for the occasion. Can you spot these costumed horses around the celebration?

Mermaid

Jester

Princess

Greek god

Pirate

Genie

Can-can dancer

Aurora and her horse, Buttercup, are visiting Flora, Fauna, and Merryweather. They think that Buttercup looks best in pink! As the fairies perform their magic, search the garden for these other things they've turned pink.

Flower

Cake

Cup

Cloak

Hat

Bow

Basket

Jasmine and her horse, Midnight, are racing Aladdin and the Genie. Their course has taken them through the marketplace, where they've managed to cause quite a mess. Look around the stalls for this topsy-turvy merchandise.

This drum

This basket of apples

This cloth

This vase

This pot

These dates

This rug

Ariel is throwing a birthday beach party for her horse, Beau. Many of Prince Eric's loyal subjects have come out to join in the celebration. Do you see these gifts they've brought for the birthday horse?

This present

Saddle

New horseshoes

Basket of treats

This gift box

Brush

Blanket

Snow White and her horse, Astor, are having a picnic with the Prince and the Dwarfs. Their blankets are full of delicious things to eat ... and there's plenty for Astor, too! Do you see these foods a horse would especially enjoy?

Apple

Carrots

Bran

Oats

Corn

Sugar cubes

Hay

Horse treat

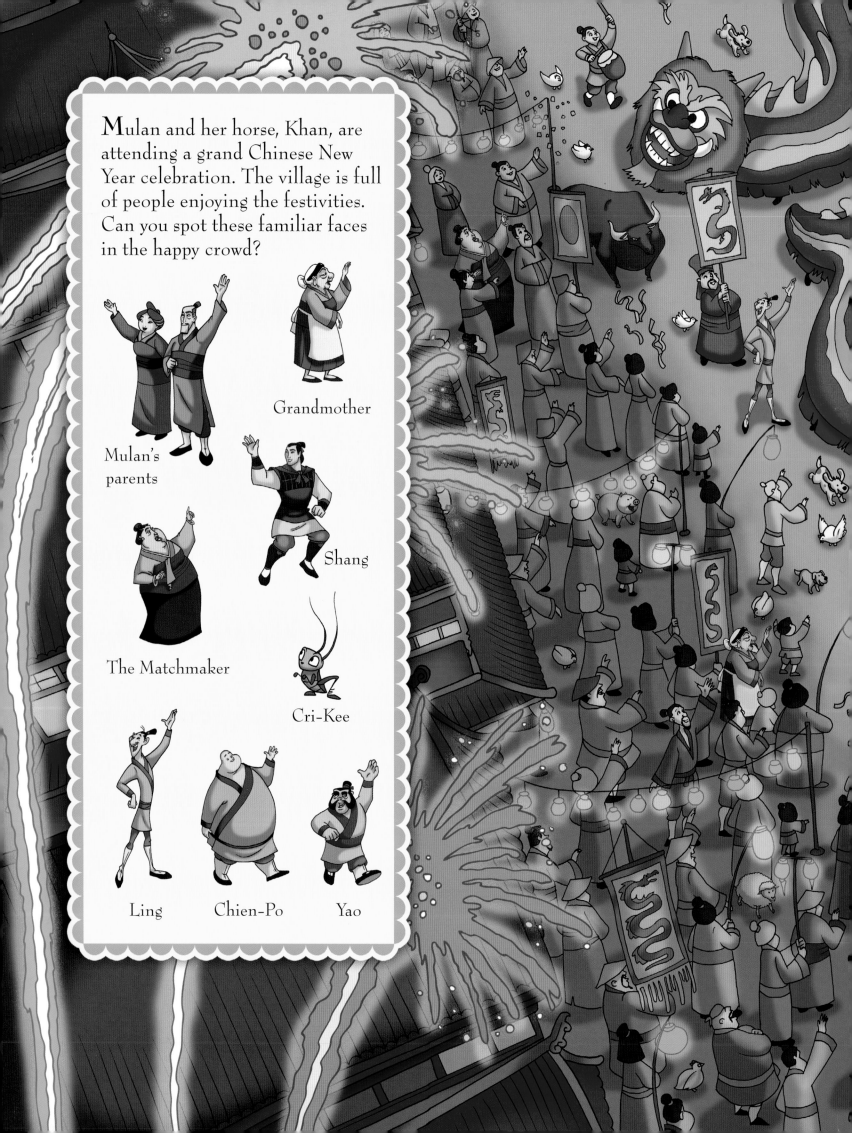

Mulan and her horse, Khan, are attending a grand Chinese New Year celebration. The village is full of people enjoying the festivities. Can you spot these familiar faces in the happy crowd?

Mulan's parents

Grandmother

The Matchmaker

Shang

Cri-Kee

Ling

Chien-Po

Yao

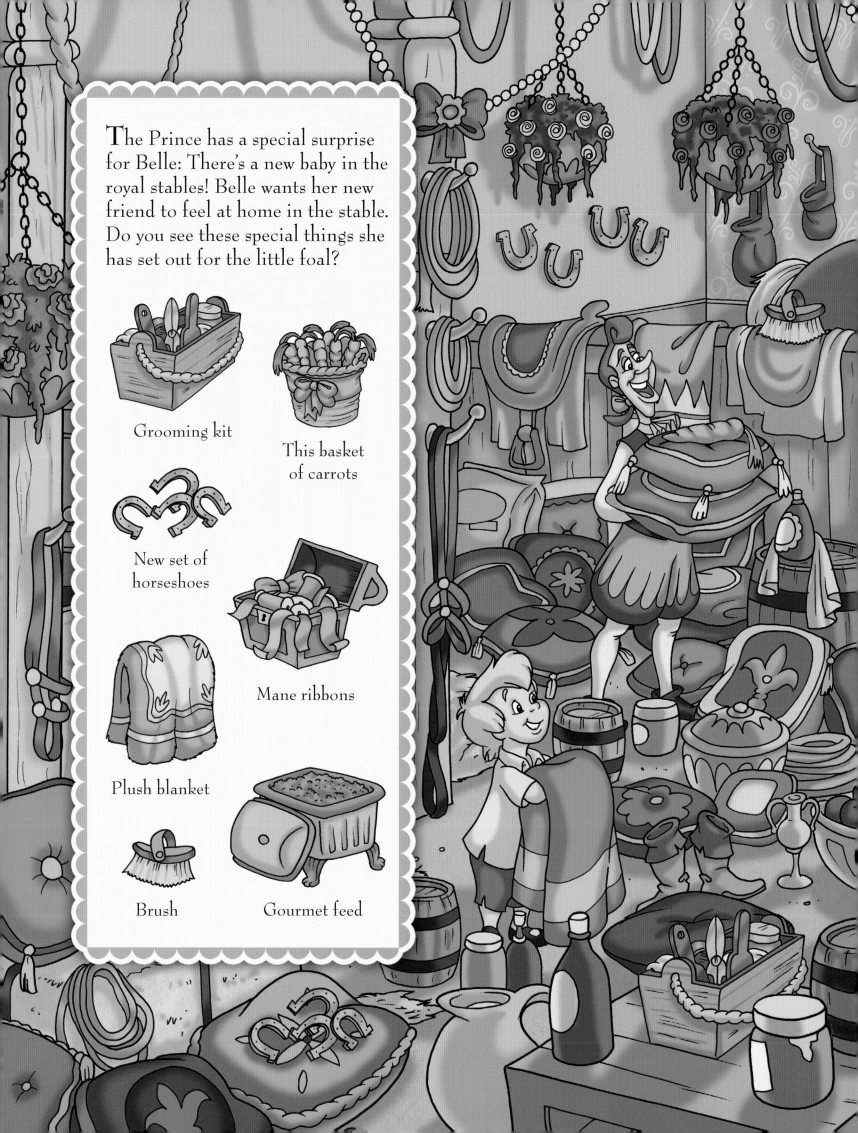

The Prince has a special surprise for Belle: There's a new baby in the royal stables! Belle wants her new friend to feel at home in the stable. Do you see these special things she has set out for the little foal?

Grooming kit

This basket of carrots

New set of horseshoes

Mane ribbons

Plush blanket

Brush

Gourmet feed

Jump back to the Royal Horse Show and look for these other proud horse owners.

The horses' costumes were popular choices at the Mardi Gras parade. Ride back and search for these revelers wearing the same costumes the horses are.

Pirate   Genie   Mermaid

Jester   Can-can dancer   Princess   Greek god

Gallop back to the good fairies' garden and look for these colorful animals.

Bunny   Frog   Cardinal

Bluebird

Deer   Skunk   Bird

Race back to the Agrabah marketplace and search for these sellers and shoppers surprised by the racers.

Some of Ariel's other animal friends have come out to celebrate Beau's birthday. Canter back to the beach party and look for these guests.

Max

Flounder

Sebastian

Cat

Dolphin

Scuttle

Dog

Amble back to the picnic and look for these delicious treats Snow White and the Dwarfs are enjoying.

Sandwich

Grapes

Salad

Sausage

Lemonade

Chicken

Cookies

Cake

In China, different animals are celebrated at the start of the new year ... including the horse! Trot back to the New Year festivities and find these other animals celebrated in China.

Dog

Dragon

Rooster

Snake

Tiger

Sheep

Pig

Ox

Head back to the stable and count 10 purple pillows Belle has used to decorate the foal's new home.